OBEY, DON'T STRAY

Lyrics by Mark Collier, David Sparks

Illustrated by Cesar E. De Castro

Painted by Kathy W. Kim

Designed by Barry K. Haun

© 2001 Little Star Entertainment
  West Covina, California 91791

Published by the Character Building Company
West Covina, California 91791
www.characterbuilding.com
ISBN 1-931454-08-6

Printed in Korea
Library of Congress cataloging-in-publication data is available from the publisher.

Songs in this book are from the **Character Classic** series and are available on cassette and CD. **Coming soon the video series.**

OBEY, DON'T STRAY

Created By

Tony Salerno

Obey, Don't Stray

Tales from the Vienna Woods - J. Strauss

"Stay in the yard;
Don't stray away,"
Said Little Tim to Pup one day.
But Pup would not
Obey Tim's words,
And wandered off to see the world.
Around the corner,
Came a van,
A dog catcher, with net in hand.
"Oh, no!" said Pup, "I'm doomed!

I disobeyed and woe is me,
Disobeyed and now I see;
I'm so upset!
Here comes the net!
Better run to my yard,
Obedience is not that hard,
When you see a dog catcher's net start to fall on your head!

Obey, Obey
I will obey
Stay in the yard,
I will not stray,
I'll follow Tim's
Advice for me,
Stay in the yard, I'll not run free."

"Stay in the yard;
Don't stray away.
I hope you've learned
How to obey.
Stay in the yard, indeed."

"I learned my lesson, yes, sir-ee!
Learned my lesson to stay free!
I'm safe today
I now obey
Little Tim, I'll be like you,
Do the things you tell me to
Little Pup will not stray,
I have learned to obey.
Little Tim, I'll be like you,
Do the things you tell me to
Little Pup will not stray,
I have learned to obey."

Now picture this song as you read or sing along...

"Stay in the yard;
Don't stray away,"
Said Little Tim to Pup one day.

But Pup would not
Obey Tim's words,

And wandered off to see the world.

Around the corner,
Came a van,

A dog catcher, with net in hand.

"Oh, no!" said Pup, "I'm doomed!
I disobeyed and woe is me,

Disobeyed and now I see;
I'm so upset!

Here comes the net!

Better run to my yard,
Obedience is not that hard,

When you see a dog catcher's net start to fall on your head!

Obey, Obey
I will obey

Stay in the yard,
I will not stray,

I'll follow Tim's
Advice for me,

Stay in the yard, I'll not run free."

"Stay in the yard;
Don't stray away.

I hope you've learned
How to obey.

Stay in the yard, indeed."

"I learned my lesson, yes, sir-ee!
Learned my lesson to stay free!

I'm safe today
I now obey

Little Tim, I'll be like you,
Do the things you tell me to

Little Pup will not stray,
I have learned to obey.

Little Tim, I'll be like you,
Do the things you tell me to

Little Pup will not stray,
I have learned to obey."

In One Ear and Out the Other

Anvil Chorus from Il Trovatore

Giuseppe Verdi

My mother told me to take off my rain boots,
Before I come in through the kitchen door,
Next thing I know down the hallway I go
With a trail of mud right across the floor,
Why don't I listen?
Before it's too late?

Things go inside one ear and then right out the other,
Why is it always hard to listen to my mother?
She knows what's best, obedience.
She makes it so clear, it goes in one ear and out the other.

My mother told me to put on my jacket,
I run out the door saying, "I'll be fine,"
Next thing I know I'm in bed with a cold,
Runny nose and a fever of ninety-nine,
Why don't I listen?
Before it's too late?

Things go inside one ear and then right out the other,
Why is it always hard to listen to my mother?
She knows what's best, obedience.
She makes it so clear, it goes in one ear and out the other.

My mother told me to do all my homework,
Before I go out with my friends to play,
Next thing I know is I have to stay home,
And do all of my homework on Saturday,
Why don't I listen?
Before it's too late?

Things go inside one ear, don't let them out the other,
Let's try obedience, and listen to your mother,
She knows what's best, obedience,
She makes it so clear, it goes in one ear, not out the other.

Little Willy, Will He?

Gypsy Rondo

Joseph Haydn

Little Willy, Little Willy, he would not obey,
And he would not follow all the rules when he would play.
Oh, he pushed and shoved and shoved and pushed
And pushed and shoved and shoved and pushed and
No one liked to play with Little Willy, Little Will.

Little Willy, Little Willy, he would not obey,
And he would not do as he was told, "I want my way!"
Oh, he disobeyed, "I want my way!"
He disobeyed, "I want my way!"
And no one liked to play with Little Willy, Little Will.

Little Willy
Will he, will he
Learn to obey
When he is at play?
Little Will if you obey,
Then others will want to play
With you, yes, it's true

Little Willy
Will he, will he
Learn to obey
When he is at play?
And if you'll follow all the rules at school
And not insist you get your way
Obey! Obey!

Little Willy, Little Will
He now obeys!
"Such a wonderful, delightful boy,"
Others will say!

Little Will, it's such a thrill
He now obeys whene'er he plays!
Oh, Little Will, you now obey
And yes, with you we want to play!

Little Will, it's such a thrill
He now obeys whene'er he plays!
Oh, Little Will, you now obey
And yes, with you we want to play!

Oh, Little Will, we want to play with you
We want to play with you, o-bey!

Happy Jack

Long Long Ago

Thomas Haynes Bayly

I have a dog, Happy Jack is his name,
How could he be so hard to train?
Must have a wire shorting out in his brain,
My little dog, Happy Jack.

Tell him to fetch, Happy Jack wants to stay,
Tell him to sit, Happy Jack runs away,
When will my dog ever learn to obey?
My little dog, Happy Jack.

Told Happy Jack 'stay away from the trash!'
Then in the night, heard such a crash,
Out from the pile he arose in a flash,
My little dog, Happy Jack.

Tell him to fetch, Happy Jack wants to stay,
Tell him to sit, Happy Jack runs away,
When will my dog ever learn to obey?
My little dog, Happy Jack.

Told Happy Jack 'see a cat, let her be!'
There Happy sat, smiling at me,
Next day he chased twenty cats up a tree,
My little dog, Happy Jack.

Tell him to fetch, Happy Jack wants to stay,
Tell him to sit, Happy Jack runs away,
When will my dog ever learn to obey?
My little dog, Happy Jack.

Took Happy Jack to obedience school,
That's where he learned every rule,
Now people think that my doggie is cool,
My little dog, Happy Jack.

Now he can fetch,
Shake a paw and play dead,
Roll over twice, even stand on his head,
Turns out the lights, even makes his own bed,
My little dog, Happy Jack.

Here is a lesson for you and for me,
It's good advice and I hope you agree,
We need to live more obediently,
Just like the dog, Happy Jack,
Just like the dog, Happy Jack,
My little dog, Happy Jack.

Stop, Look at the Sign!
Sonatina in C Major
William Duncombe

Stop, look at the sign,
Do what it says because it's there to help you,
Stop, make up your mind,
Study it close, obey the sign!
Stop, look at the sign,
Giving important information to you,
Stop, make up your mind,
Do what it says, obey the sign.

'Warning,' 'Caution,' 'Stay Away,'
'Don't Feed the Animals Today,'
These are the signs, we will obey them,
Everywhere we go.

'Wait' and 'Yield,' and 'Stop' and 'Go,'
There's 'Walk' and 'Don't Walk,' 'Fast' and 'Slow' and
'Right Turn,' 'Left Turn,' 'Open,' 'Closed,'
To help the traffic flow- so,

Stop, look at the sign,
Do what it says because it's there to help you,
Stop, make up your mind,
Study it close, obey the sign!
Stop, look at the sign,
Giving important information to you,
Stop, make up your mind,
Do what it says, obey the sign.

Every sign is for a reason,
'Danger,' 'Keep Out,' 'Hunting Season'
'No Trespassing' on a tree then,
Go back where you came from.

By the lake it says 'Thin Ice'
'Beware of Dog' is good advice,
Obey the sign, or pay the price,
Now you know what to do- so,

Stop! Because it's there to help you,
Stop! Obey the sign.
Stop! Important information to you
Stop! Obey the sign.

Stop, look at the sign,
Do what it says because it's there to help you,
Stop, make up your mind,
Study it close, obey the sign!
Stop, look at the sign,
Giving important information to you,
Stop, make up your mind,
Do what it says, obey...

Stop! Obey the sign.

Fine.

fee´nay

A musical term for the end.